Welcome, Little Baby

Aliki

GREENWILLOW BOOKS, NEW YORK

Printed in Hong Kong
by South China Printing Co.
First Edition 10 9 8 7 6 5 4 3 2 1

The full-color art was done in watercolor,
crayon, and ink. The typeface is ITC Galliard.

Library of Congress
Cataloging-in-Publication Data

Aliki. Welcome, little baby.
Summary: A mother welcomes her newborn infant, and
tells what life will be like as the child grows older.
[1. Babies—Fiction. 2. Mother and child—Fiction]
I. Title. PZ7.A397Wg 1987 [E] 86-7648
ISBN 0-688-06810-3 ISBN 0-688-06811-1 (lib. bdg.)

Welcome, Nichola Huffman

Welcome to our world, little baby.
We've been waiting for you.

You're very small

and all you want is

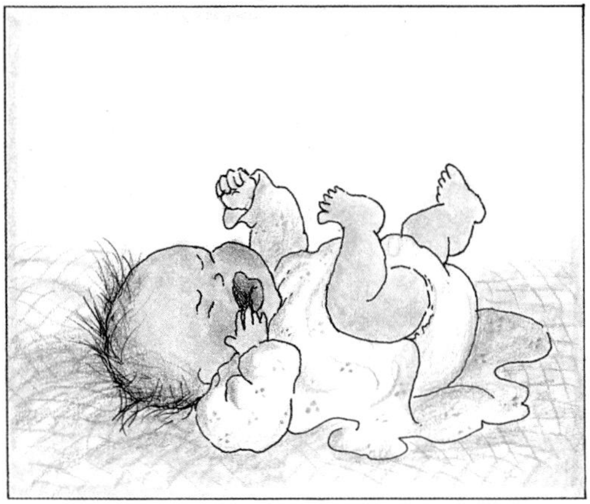

to eat,

to sleep,

and to feel warm.

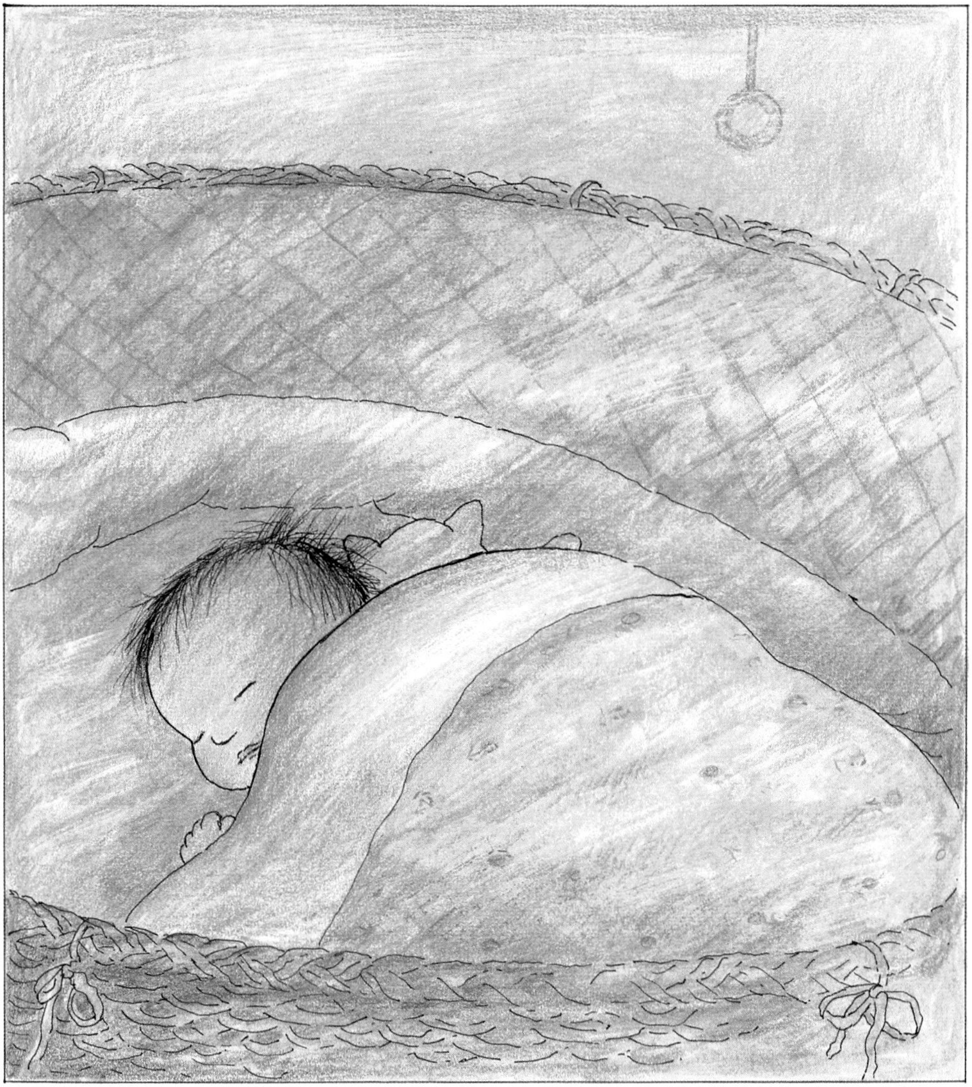

You will grow and grow

and find the world around you.

You'll see it.

You'll smell it, and feel it, too.

You'll hear sounds

you never heard before.

You'll learn to walk, to run,

to talk, to read.

You'll discover things

you didn't know

when you were born.

Welcome to our world, little baby.